SIMPLY READ BOOKS

For Mom, Dad, Maryellen, Brian, John, Bobby and Joey.

The World
that Loved Books

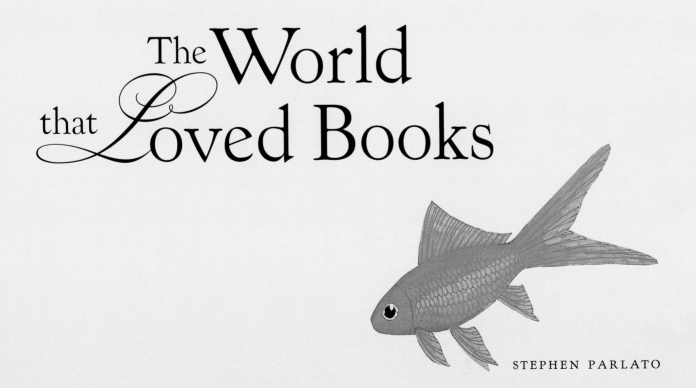

STEPHEN PARLATO

There once was a world where everyone loved books, even the animals.

Everyone loved to read so much that when they read their books, they became what they read.

A man reading about flowers...

became flowers.

A man reading about insects and bugs

became insects and bugs.

A rabbit reading about turtles

became turtles

his perfect little cottontail now a
sea turtle's flipper.

A cat reading about mice, rats & hamsters

soon had many tales to tell

A woman reading about angels

became choirs of angels.

A dragon reading about treasure became a treasure of gold and diamonds and pearls.

He felt all polished and shiny and new.

A man reading about snakes and lizards
found it s‑s‑s‑s‑s‑s‑so s‑s‑s‑s‑scientific, he
thought it was

s‑s‑s‑s‑simply terrific.

A dinosaur reading about

frogs and salamanders

became

frogs &
salamanders.

He found the book to be very ribbiting.

A woman reading about birds in a
lightning storm

became

birds fleeing a

storm.

A rhinoceros reading about butterflies and caterpillars
grew so many

beautiful wings

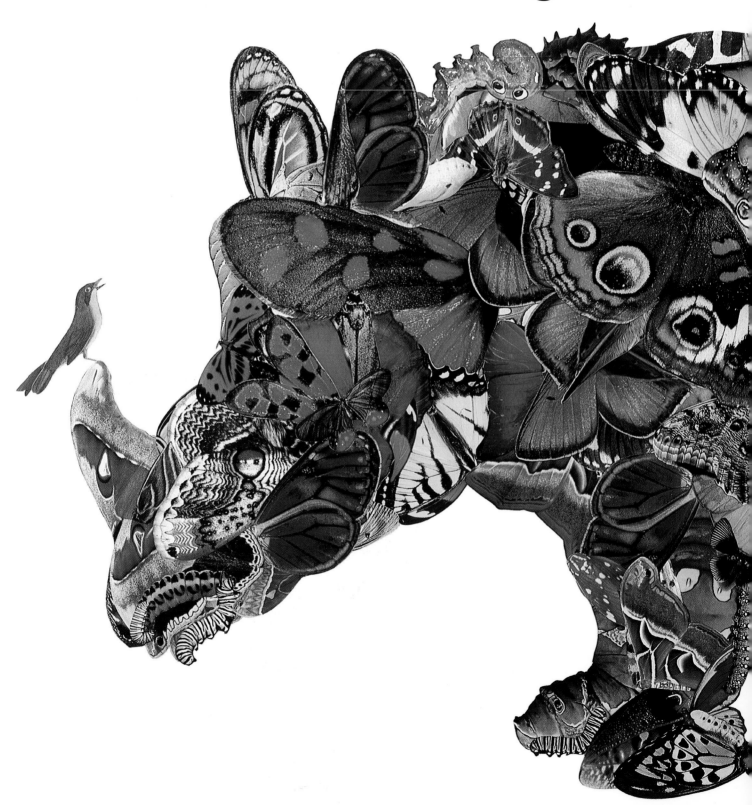

that it made his friend the little bird quite jealous.

When the man's friend, a horse,
borrowed his book about snakes and lizards,

it simply gave him the shivers.

The horse who had read the book about
fish enjoyed it so much, she decided to buy a
copy as a present and sent it to her friend.

Who found it a
swimmingly
good read.

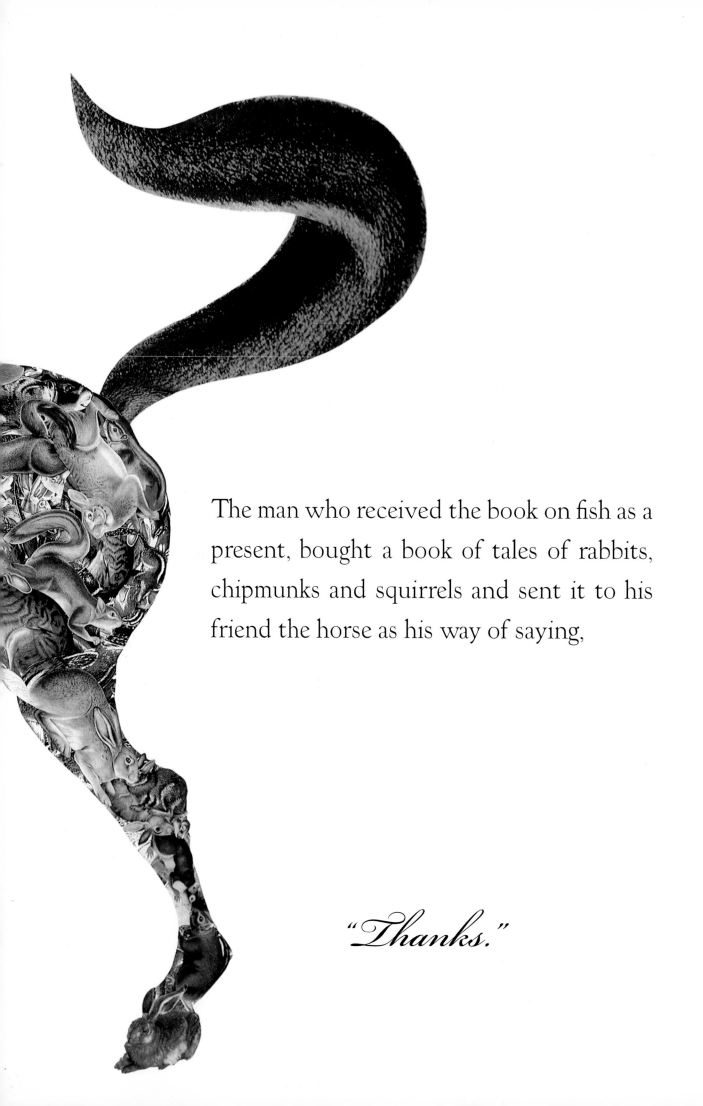

The man who received the book on fish as a present, bought a book of tales of rabbits, chipmunks and squirrels and sent it to his friend the horse as his way of saying,

"Thanks."

The horse then wanted to read more,
so she went to the public library
and borrowed a book
about flags.

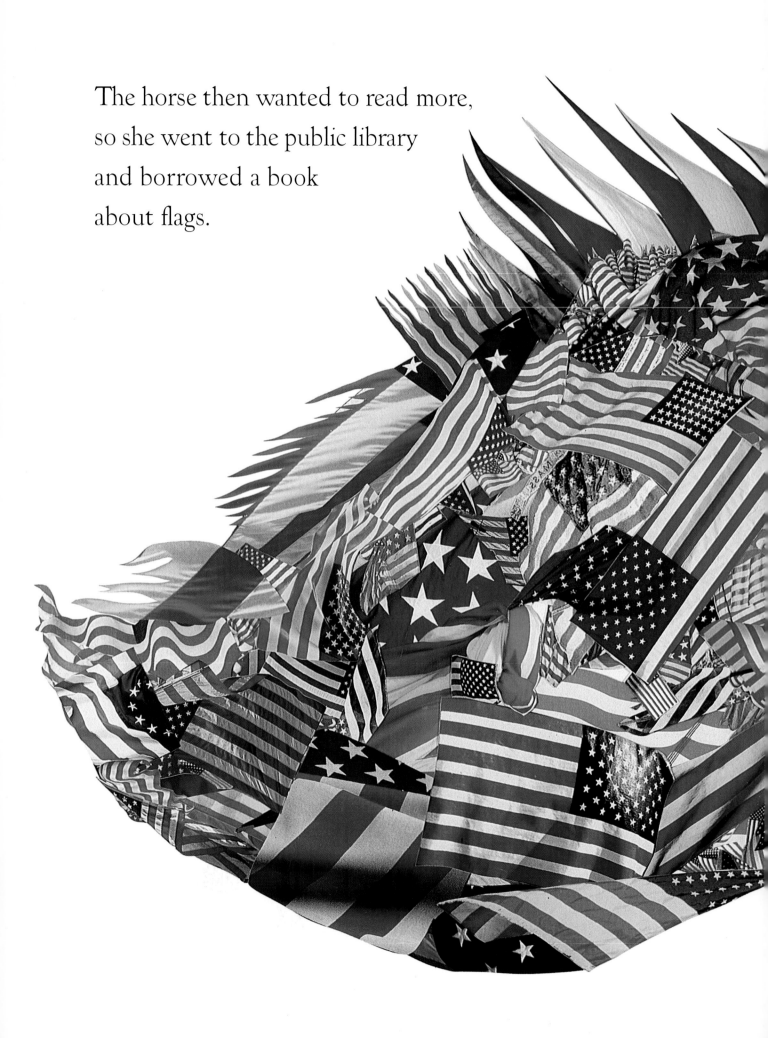

She was feeling so proud, waving even at strangers.

She was one day late returning the
book and had to pay a fine.

The End

The World that Loved Books

TEXT & ILLUSTRATION © 2004 STEPHEN PARLATO

ALL RIGHTS RESERVED. NO PART OF THIS PUBLICATION MAY BE
REPRODUCED, STORED IN A RETRIEVAL SYSTEM, OR TRANSMITTED,
IN ANY FORM OR BY ANY MEANS, ELECTRONIC, MECHANICAL,
PHOTOCOPYING, RECORDING OR OTHERWISE, WITHOUT WRITTEN
PERMISSION OF THE PUBLISHER.

CATALOGUING IN PUBLICATION DATA

PARLATO, STEPHEN, 1954‑
  THE WORLD THAT LOVED BOOKS/STEPHEN PARLATO.

ISBN 1‑894965‑04‑3

  I.BOOKS AND READING‑‑JUVENILE FICTION.I.TITLE.
PZ7.P23W02003   J813'.6   C2003‑910263‑7

FIRST PUBLISHED BY SIMPLY READ BOOKS
501‑5525 W. BOULEVARD, VANCOUVER BC V6M 3W6

PRINTED AND BOUND IN ITALY BY GRAFICHE AZ, VERONA

10   9   8   7   6   5   4   3   2